THE VILLAGE GARAGE

G. Brian Karas

Christy Ottaviano Books

HENRY HOLT AND COMPANY ✺ NEW YORK

AUTHOR'S NOTE

The village in *The Village Garage* is fictional. It closely resembles the one I live near,
except for an extra hill here or a turn in the road there. I want to thank George Wyant
and the crew at the Rhinebeck Village Garage for their help with this book and their
hard work around town.

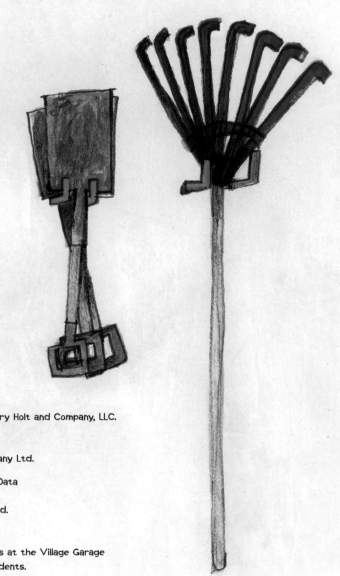

Henry Holt and Company, LLC
Publishers since 1866
175 Fifth Avenue
New York, New York 10010
www.HenryHoltKids.com

Library of Congress Cataloging-in-Publication Data
Karas, G. Brian.
The Village Garage / by G. Brian Karas. — 1st ed.
p.   cm.
"Christy Ottaviano Books."
Summary: Throughout the seasons the workers at the Village Garage
are busy taking care of the town and its residents.
ISBN 978-0-8050-8716-1
[1. Garages—Fiction. 2. Seasons—Fiction. 3. City and town life—Fiction.] I. Title.
PZ7.K1296Vi 2010   [E]—dc22   2009009223

First Edition—2010 / Designed by April Ward
The illustrations for this book were created with gouache and acrylic with pencil on Arches paper.
Printed in October 2009 in China by C&C Joint Printing Co., Shenzhen, Guangdong Province, on acid-free paper. ∞

10 9 8 7 6 5 4 3 2 1

9

For Paige,
with love

Cherry ST

SPEED
25

STOP

2 HOUR
PARKING

9 AM-
5 PM

1 HOUR
PARKING

9 AM-
3 PM

It's SPRING and that means
the workers at the Village
Garage are busy cleaning up.

There are sticks from winter storms,
sand from snowplows,
and leftover leaves from autumn.

Out come the rakes
and street sweepers.

Out comes the wood chipper.

"Mulch for sale," says George, the boss.

The sun is shining and a warm south wind blows.

It's a good day to wash the trucks.

Now for a little fun.

SPLASH

"Hey!"

It's nearly **SUMMER**. Lots of cars
will soon be on the road. Time to patch
the potholes and fill the cracks.

"More tar, Mike!" hollers John.
Fill the holes, roll and roll.

A summer thunderstorm washes out
a bridge and knocks down phone lines.

Out come shovels,
picks, and a backhoe.
Fix the **bridge!**
Fix the **lines!**

It's the Fourth of July, and the Village Garage has a party.

Hot dogs! Fireworks!
Free rides on the
front-end loader!

On the fifth of July, George says,
"Back to work."

"Boo!" groan the crew.
But George knows they're joking.

It's time to paint new
road stripes, pick up the
garbage, and mow the grass.
Summer is a busy season.

The wind soon changes and blows in from
the north. It's AUTUMN. Leaves turn
from green to yellow and red, then brown.

And they fall.
EVERYWHERE.

RRRRRRRRWWWWWHHHHHHHH
SSSSSHHHHHHHH
SSSS HHHHH
SSSO OOO
OOOOOOOOOO

Get out the Elephant Truck!
(That's what they call the big machine
that sucks up the leaves.)

"You missed one," yells Scott.

"**WHAT?**" yells Bob.

"**YOU MISSED A LEAF!**" yells Scott, again.

"**WHAT?**" yells Bob, again.

The Elephant Truck is a noisy machine, but it gets the job done.

At last, the leaves are gone, and the crew take a break. "No time to rest," says George. "There's a broken pipe in the Village Hall—water all over the place!"

Back to work.

WINTER is here, and a big snowstorm is moving in. The crew get ready. They load the trucks with sand and salt. They take out the snow shovels.

The crew wait. And wait. Chris starts a card game.

Tony sings in the karaoke machine. John plays the drums.

"Finally!" someone says
when the storm starts.

The snow piles up quickly.

It's time for the trucks to roll out.

CHINK CHINK CHINK, the chains rattle.
KKKKKKRRRRRRRRRRR, the plows scrape.
SWSSSSSSSSHHHH! SWSSSSSSSSHHHH!
The sand and salt spray, and the trucks
rumble in the muffled night.

By morning the roads are clear.
Out come the sleds.

They all make a snowman.

VILLAGE
GARAGE

Look out—
SNOWBALLS!

And then they wait for
the next storm to blow in.
"I sure wish spring would
come," says George.

And it does!